The Saucy Jane Family

Also available in the *Family* series by **Enid Blyton**

The Buttercup Farm Family
The Caravan Family
The Pole Star Family
The Queen Elizabeth Family
The Seaside Family

Also by **Enid Blyton**

Amelia Jane Again!
Amelia Jane Gets Into Trouble!
Naughty Amelia Jane!
Amelia Jane is Naughty Again!
Five O'Clock Tales
Six O'Clock Tales
Seven O'Clock Tales
Eight O'Clock Tales
The Adventures of the Wishing-Chair
The Wishing-Chair Again
The Magic Faraway Tree
The Folk of the Faraway Tree
The Enchanted Wood

The *Malory Towers* series
The *Mystery* series
The *St Clare's* series

Enid Blyton

The Saucy Jane Family

R. GERVIS

mammoth

First published in Great Britain 1947
by Lutterworth Press

Published 1991 by Mammoth
Reissued 1997 by Mammoth,
an imprint of Reed International Books Ltd
Michelin House, 81 Fulham Road, London SW3 6RB
and Auckland and Melbourne

ISBN 0 7497 0805 0

10 9 8 7 6 5 4 3 2 1

A CIP catalogue record for this title
is available from the British Library.

CONTENTS

1   A MOST EXCITING IDEA

MIKE, Belinda and Ann were three lucky
children. They were at school all the
week—and from Friday to Monday they lived
in a caravan!

Mummy and Daddy lived in one caravan and
the three children had the other. It was such
fun. In the holidays they went to visit Uncle
Ned and Aunt Clara. Then their two good
horses, Davey and Clopper, pulled the caravans down
many little winding lanes to Uncle Ned's
farm.

"It's lovely to have a house on wheels!"
cried Mike, when he sat at the front of his
caravan and drove Clopper steadily on. "I
wouldn't like to live in a house that always
stood still."

When the summer holidays came, Daddy wondered whether they should all go to the sea.
"Our caravans want cleaning and painting," he
said. "The stove wants something done to it,
too."

"Oh, Daddy—must we go and stay in a
house!" said Ann, who, now that she had lived
in a caravan on wheels, didn't like living in a

7

house at all. "Can't we take the caravans with us?"

"No. We really must get them properly cleaned up," said Daddy. "I'd like to take you to the sea, because you must learn to swim, and to handle a boat. All children should know how to swim."

"I'd like to," said Mike. "I'd like to dive as well. And swim under water like a fish. I've seen people doing it."

It was very difficult to get rooms by the sea anywhere, because Daddy had left it rather late. He tried to hire a cara- van by the sea, too, but

they were all taken. It really seemed as if the children wouldn't be able to go.

And then one day Mummy had a most exciting letter. She read it to herself first, and her eyes shone.

"Listen!" she said. "I wonder how you would like this children?"

"What?" cried the three of them and Daddy looked up from his newspaper.

"It's a letter from an old friend of mine,"

said Mummy. "She has a houseboat on a canal not very far from here—and she says she will lend it to us for the holidays if we like."

"A houseboat?" said Ann, in wonder. "What's that? Does she mean a boat-house —where boats are kept?

Everyone laughed. "Isn't Ann a baby?" said Mike. "Silly, it's a proper boat that people *live* in—they make their home there, just as we make ours in the caravan."

"Do they?" said Ann. "Do they really live on the boat all day and night? Oh Mummy, I'd like to see a houseboat."

"And I'd simply LOVE to live in one!" said Belinda. "Oh, I would! To hear the water all day and night, and so see fish jumping —and the little moorhens swimming about. Oh, Mummy!"

"Where this houseboat?" said Daddy. "It certainly does sound rather exciting."

"It's at Mayberry," said Mummy. "On the canal there. It's a very pretty part, I know. It's a lovely houseboat—big enough to take all of us quite comfortably."

"What's the boat called?" asked Mike. "Does the letter say, Mummy?"

"Yes. It's called *Saucy Jane*," said Mummy, smiling. "What a funny name!"

"It's a *lovely* name!" said Belinda. "I like

it. The *Saucy Jane*. We shan't be the Caravan
Family—we shall be the Family of the *Saucy Jane*."

"Let's go to-day," said Ann. "Mummy, can
we?"

"Of course not," said Mummy. "You can't
do things all in a hurry like that. Daddy has
got to arrange about the caravans being done—
and we must find out what we can do with
Davey and Clopper."

"Oh, Mummy—we can't leave Davey and
Clopper behind." cried Mike. "You know we
can't. They would be awfully miserable."

"Well, we can't have horses living on a boat,"
said Daddy. "Be sensible, Mike."

"They could live in a nearby field," said
Mike. He loved Davey and Clopper with all
his heart, and looked after them well.

"We'll see," said Daddy. "They might perhaps be useful to us if we wanted to go up the
canal a little way in the houseboat."

"Oh—would Davey and Clopper pull our
boat?" cried Ann. "Wouldn't they feel odd,
pulling a boat instead of a caravan?"

"Well—what about it, Daddy?" said Mummy,
still looking rather excited. "Shall we try a
holiday on a houseboat? The children could
learn to swim and dive, and they could learn
to handle a little boat too. Just what we want
them to do."

"It does seem as if we were meant to go," said Daddy, smiling. "We can't get in anywhere by the sea—so a river or a canal is the next best thing. Yes write to your friend and tell her we'll go and see the *Saucy Jane*."

"And we'll make up our minds whether to live in it for the holidays or not when we see it," said Mummy.

"I'm going to tell Davey and Clopper all about it," said Ann, and she ran off to where the two big horses stood close together in the field.

"Don't be long," called Mummy. "It's almost time to go to bed."

But when they were in their bunks in the caravan that night, the three children couldn't go to sleep for a long time. They talked about the *Saucy Jane*, they planned what they would do—and when at last they did fall asleep they dreamt about her too.

The *Saucy Jane!* What would she be like? Just as nice as a Caravan—perhaps nicer!

THE *SAUCY JANE*

NEXT morning at breakfast-time all the family talked about when they could go and see the *Saucy Jane*.

"The sooner the better, I think," said Daddy. "What about to-day? There's a bus that goes quite near Mayberry. We could catch it and walk across the field to the canal."

"Oh, Daddy—to-day!" said Belinda. "Yes, let's go to-day. It's such a lovely day."

So when they had washed up the breakfast things, tidied the caravans, and locked the doors, they all set off. They caught the bus at the corner of the lane and settled down for a fairly long ride.

"What is a canal Daddy? Is it a river?" asked Ann.

"Oh, no," said Daddy. "A canal is made by man—cut out by machinery, and filled with water. It is usually very straight, but if it meets a hill it goes round it."

"Doesn't it ever go through it?" asked Mike.

"Yes, sometimes. Some canals go through quite long tunnels," said Daddy; "a mile, two miles or more."

"Do fishes live in canal water—and wild birds?" asked Belinda.

"Oh, yes," said Daddy, "They are old now, these canals we have made all over the country, and to you they will look just like rivers. They have weeds growing in them, fish of many kinds, wild birds on the banks. Trees lean over the sides, fields come right down to the canals, though where they run through towns there are houses by them, of course."

"Why did we build canals, when we have so many rivers?" asked Mike.

"Well, many goods were sent by water in the old days, when goods had to be taken about all over the country, and the roads were bad, and the railways were only just beginning," said Daddy. "But rivers wind about too much—so straight canals were cut."

"I see," said Mike. "I suppose big boats were loaded in the towns, and then they were taken across the country to other big towns—by canal."

"Yes," said Daddy. "I'll show you the boats that take them—canal-boats and barges. You'll see plenty going by if we live on the houseboat."

"*If!* You mean *when!*" cried Belinda. "Are we nearly there, Daddy? I want to see the canal and the *Saucy Jane*. I can't wait another minute."

But she had to wait, because the bus was not yet near Mayberry. At last it stopped at a little inn and the bus conductor called to Daddy.

"This is where you get out, sir. You'll find the canal across those fields there. You can just see it from here."

They all got out. They climbed the stile and walked across a cornfield by a narrow path right through the middle of the whispering corn. The corn was as high as Ann, and she liked looking through the forest of tall green stalks.

They crossed another field and then came to the canal. It was, as Daddy had said, very like an ordinary river. Trees and bushes overhung the opposite side, but the cornfield went right down to the edge of the side they were on.

The canal stretched as far as they could see, blue and straight. A little way up it, on the opposite side, were two or three big white boats —houseboats, with people living in them. Smoke rose from the chimney of one of them.

"There are the boats," said Mummy. "I wonder which is the *Saucy Jane*! Dear me, Daddy, how are we going to get across'"

"Borrow a little boat and row it!" said Daddy. "Come along!"

They were soon just opposite the house-boats. One was very colourful indeed, with red geraniums and blue lobelias planted in pots and

baskets all round the sitting-space on the little roof.

"I do hope that's the *Saucy Jane*," said

Belinda to Ann. "It's much the nicest. It's so shining white, too!"

There was a small cottage by the canal, and

a woman was in the garden hanging out clothes. Daddy called to her. "Is the *Saucy Jane* over there! Can we get to her in a boat?"

"Yes, that's the Saucy Jane," said the woman. "The boat with the geraniums. She's got a little boat belonging to her, but I expect it's moored beside her. You're welcome to borrow my boat, if you like. It's the little dinghy down beside you."

"Thank you," said Daddy.

Everyone got in, Daddy untied the rope and took the oars. Over the water they went to the *Saucy Jane*. Somebody came out on deck, appearing from the cabin-part in the middle.

Mummy gave a cry of delight. "Molly! You're here! We've come to see the boat!"

"Oh, what fun!" cried Mummy's friend. "I never expected you so soon. Look, tie your dinghy just there—and climb up."

In great excitement the children climbed up on the spotless deck. So this was the *Saucy Jane*—a house on a boat! They looked at the cabin-part; proper doors led into it, two doors, painted white with a little red line round the panels.

There were chairs on deck to sit in and watch the boats that went by. There were even chairs on the roof-part, up by the geraniums and lobelias. Ann didn't know which to do first—climb up on the roof by the little iron ladder, or go into the exciting-looking cabin.

"Come along and I'll show you over the

Saucy Jane," said Mummy's friend, smiling. "You can call me Auntie Molly. When you've seen everything, we'll sit down and have some biscuits and lemonade, and talk about whether you'd like to have a holiday here."

"We would, we would!" said all three children together. "We've made up our minds already!"

R·GERVIS.

3. WHAT FUN TO BE ON A HOUSEBOAT!

IT was very exciting to explore the big houseboat. Down in the cabin-part there were two bedrooms and a small living-room. There was even a tiny kitchen, very clean and neat, with just room to take about two steps in!

In one room there was no bed, though Auntie Molly said it was a bedroom. In the other room there were bunks for beds, just as there were in the caravan—two on one side of the wall, and a third that could be folded up into the wall on the other side.

"I call that bunk my spare-room," said Auntie Molly, with a laugh. "I can sleep three people in this bedroom and two in the other."

"But where do they sleep in the other room?" asked Mike, puzzled. "I didn't see any bed at all."

"Oh, I forgot to show it to you," said Auntie Molly. "It's really rather clever, the way it comes out of the wall. Come and see."

She took them back into the other cabin bedroom, and went to the wall at the back.

There was a handle there and she pulled it. Out came a double bed, opening itself like a concertina! Auntie Molly pulled down four short legs, and hey presto! There was the bed. Tucked away in another cupboard were blankets, sheets and mattress.

"It's like magic," said Ann. "And isn't it a good idea ? It would take up a lot of room if you had the bed standing all day in this little room. Can I push it back, please?"

It was as easy to push back into the wall as it was to pull out.

"That will be Mummy's and Daddy's bed," said Belinda. "Auntie Molly, this houseboat is just right for our family, you know—you've got beds or bunks for five people."

"Yes," said Aunt Mollie. "I knew you had been used to living in a caravan, and I thought you would be just the family to enjoy my houseboat. I was sure you would keep it clean and tidy, because I've heard how beautiful your caravans are."

"Oh, yes—we'd keep your boat spotless," said Belinda. "I would scrub down the deck each day. I'd love that. That's what sailors do, isn't it, Mummy?"

There was a stove in the tiny kitchen for cooking, and a chimney stuck out at the top of the roof for the smoke. There were neat cupboards all round the kitchen, and mugs and cups hung in neat rows.

"You can wash up in the canal water," said Aunt Mollie, "and any other washing you want to do you can do in the canal too. Drinking-water you can get from Mrs. Toms' well at the cottage opposite. I fetch it in a big water-jar."

"I can see that our jobs here will be quite different from our jobs in the caravan," said Mike, "but they will be very exciting. Daddy, can I fetch the drinking-water each day, please !"

"As soon as you can handle a boat, and can swim, you may," said Daddy.

Aunt Molly suddenly looked rather alarmed. "Oh—can't the children swim?" she said. "Then I really don't think you ought to come and live here. You see, it's so easy to fall into the water, and if you can't swim, you might drown."

The children stared at her in dismay. How dreadful if they couldn't come and live on this lovely boat just because they couldn't swim!

"We're going to learn," said Mike at once. "We're going to learn the very first day we get here. You needn't worry."

"But can the little girl learn?," asked Aunt Molly looking doubtfully at Ann. "Really, I think if you come you'll have to tie her up with a rope, so that if she does fall into the water she can drag herself back to the houseboat."

"Tie me up? Like a little dog? I won't be tied up!" cried Ann indignantly. "I've never heard of such a thing!"

"My dear child, a great many of the canal people tie their children up until they can swim," said Aunt Molly. "Now, just look what's coming by. I believe it's a canal-boat called *Happy Sue*. If it is you will see the two babies of the Happy Sue tied up with ropes. How could their parents possibly risk letting them fall in and be drowned?"

A long canal-boat came chugging by. In the middle of it was a built-up cabin, where the people lived. In the hold, where they carried goods, were great boxes which the boat was taking to the next big town. On these boxes played two small children, about two years old. They were so alike that the children guessed they were twins.

"Yes—they are tied to that post by a rope," said Belinda, in surprise. "Oh, Aunt Molly, what a pretty boat—it's all painted with castles and roses."

"All the canal-boats are painted like that," said Aunt Molly. "The canal-people have their own ways and customs. You must make friends with some of the children and let them tell you all about their unusual life. They are always on the move, sailing up and down the canals they know so well."

The canal-boat went by, and behind it were two barges full of coal, which the first boat was pulling along. The *Saucy Jane* bobbed up and down a little as the big boats went by and sent waves rippling to the banks.

"Oh!—Now the Saucy Jane really does feel like a boat!" said Ann, delighted. "She was so still before, she might have been on land. But now she's bobbing like a real boat. I like it."

"Now for biscuits and lemonade," said Aunt Molly. "And we'll decide when you're to come. I move out to-morrow. You can come any time after that."

"The very next day!" shouted Mike. "Mummy, can we? The very next day !"

And Mummy nodded her head. "Yes, we'll come on Thursday. We really will."

4.   SETTLING IN

THE children went back to their caravans in great excitement. It really seemed too good to be true, to think that they were actually going to the *Saucy Jane* on Thursday !

Daddy went to see a man in the village about painting and cleaning the caravans. A nearby farmer asked if he might borrow Davey for the holidays, to help in the harvesting. He didn't want Clopper.

"Yes, you may certainly borrow Davey," said Daddy. "He's getting too fat. He could do with some hard work. We will take Clopper with us, in case we want to go up the canal in the *Saucy Jane.*"

On Thursday a car drew up in the lane outside the field where the two caravans stood. Mummy and the children got into it with their luggage. Daddy said good-bye to them, standing by big Clopper, who looked in surprise at the waving family.

"It's all right, Clopper. Daddy is riding you all the way to the *Saucy Jane!*" called Ann. "You'll take longer than we do. We'll have everything ready for you, Daddy, when you come."

Off went the car. Daddy jumped up on Clopper's broad back, and the two jogged off down the lane. Daddy knew some short cuts, but even so it would take a long while to get to Mayberry on slow old Clopper. But who minded that on this lovely summer's day, when honeysuckle grew in the hedges, and red poppies glowed in the corn! Daddy felt very happy, and he whistled as he rode on Clopper, thinking of the *Saucy Jane*, and wondering how his little family would like their new life.

"The very first thing I must do is to teach them all to swim," he thought. "Ann doesn't like the water very much. I do hope she won't make a fuss about it. I wonder if they have reached the *Saucy Jane* yet."

They had! They were even then climbing up on her spotless deck, calling happily to one another.

"Here we are, in our new home! I hope lots of boats and barges go by so that the *Saucy Jane* bobs up and down all the time !"

"I'm going to have the top bunk. Mummy, can I have the top one? I like climbing."

"I'll always pull your bed out of the wall, Mummy, and get it ready for you at night." That was Belinda. She loved to be useful.

Living in a caravan and having to do so many odd jobs had taught her to be a very sensible little girl indeed.

Auntie Molly had left blankets, linen, crockery, knives and forks—in fact, everything they would need. Mummy said that it was even more important to keep Auntie Molly's things nice than their own.

"It is so very kind of her to lend them to us and to trust us with them," she said. "We must be extra careful not to break anything, or spoil any of her belongings. If people trust us, the least we can do is to be trustworthy!"

It was such fun unpacking their things and putting them into the drawers that lined the walls of the little cabin-bedrooms. There was even space to hang coats and dresses. Belinda went on shore to pick some flowers to fill the vase on the little table in the sitting-room.

Mummy began to cook a meal on the small stove. She had already packed away into the neat larder the food they had brought with them. She was used to the ways of a caravan, where every bit of space was used. It was just the same on the houseboat.

Soon the smell of bacon frying filled the air, and the children sniffed hungrily.

"Where's Daddy? Isn't he coming yet?" said Ann, and she went out on the deck.

Mummy called to her warningly.

"Now, Ann—don't go near the edge of the boat, in case you topple over! You're not tied up, you know."

"I can see Daddy and Clopper!" shouted Am. "Mike! Belinda! Here he comes! Look at old Clopper; he's as proud as anything to carry Daddy. Hi, Daddy, DADDY!"

Daddy had arranged with Mrs. Toms to let Clopper stay in a little field opposite the boat, where she kept a cow and a few geese. He

jumped down from the big horse's back, called
to Mrs. Toms, gave Clopper a friendly smack and
ran to the little dinghy by the bank. Clopper stared
after him. "Hrrrrumph!" he said, in surprise,
as he saw Daddy rowing off in the boat. Then
he went down to the water to have a long drink.

"Hallo, Daddy!" called the children.
"You're just in time for supper. Can you
smell the bacon?"

"Welcome to the *Saucy Jane!*" said Mummy,
appearing out of the cabin door, her face red

with cooking. "Shall we have our meal up on deck! The cabin is very tiny, and it's such a lovely evening."

"Oh, yes, yes," said Belinda. "I know where a little folding table is. I'll get it and lay it. Hurrah for supper on deck!"

Very soon they were all sitting round the low table, enjoying their first meal on the *Saucy Jane*. A little breeze ran over the water, and the boat lifted herself up and down on the ripples. Two moorhens swam by, and a fish suddenly jumped right out of the water at a fly. Swallows flew low, just skimming the canal, twittering in their sweet high voices.

"This is the loveliest place in the world," said Belinda. "Lovelier than the caravan. Oh, listen to the plash-plash of the water against the sides of the boat, Mummy."

"I do love being right at the very beginning of a holiday," said Ann, sleepily. " It's such a nice feeling. I don't want to go to bed to-night, Mummy. I want to stay up on deck for hours and hours and hours."

"Well, it's your bedtime now," said Mummy. "Hurry, and you can have the top bunk! It may be nice out here—but think of sleeping down there, with the *Saucy Jane* bobbing whenever a boat goes by. Hurry, Am. You're half asleep already!"

5.   BELINDA WAKES UP EARLY

THE first day on the *Saucy Jane* was one long delight.   Belinda awoke first and crept out of her bunk so as not to wake the others.   She went up on deck in her nightie, but it was already so warm that she was not a bit cold.

The canal stretched up and down, a soft pale blue, edged with green.   The sun was rising, and here and there gold flecks freckled the water.   The two moorhens swam by again, and a magnificent swan floated slowly up, his image reflected so beautifully in the water that he really almost looked like two swans, Belinda thought.

"One swan the right way up and the other upside down," she said to herself.   " Swan, come back at breakfast-time and I'll give you some bread."

The swan turned his head on his long, grace-full neck, gave Belinda a look, and then sailed on again.   The swallows came down to the water for flies, twittering all the time.   Belinda leaned over to look down into the water itself.

"There are hundreds and hundreds of baby fish!" she said. "All going about together.

31

How they dart about ! And there's a great big fish. He's made all the little ones hurry away. Oh, here comes a canal-boat."

The gaily-painted boat slid along—but this time it had no motor inside it to chug-chug-chug and send it through the water. Instead, to Belinda's great delight, a big horse was pulling it.

The horse walked steadily along a path on the opposite bank. A rope tied to him ran to the boat, and by this he pulled the long, heavy boat along. A girl sat by the long tiller, guiding her boat easily.

She called to Belinda, "Nice morning ! Going to be hot to-day!"

"I wish we lived on a boat like yours!" called Belinda. "Ours stays still."

"Yours is only a houseboat," cried the girl. "It's a play-boat. Ours goes to work. It's a canal-boat. We go for miles and miles. Good-bye!"

The canal-boat slid right by, sending waves to make the *Saucy Jane* bob again. The horse pulling the boat had not even turned his head. Belinda could hear the sound of his hoofs for a long time in the clear still morning air.

Mummy had heard her calling, and woke up. She looked at her little clock. Half-past five in the morning ! Whatever was Belinda doing, up so early? Mummy went up on deck, ready to scold.

"Belinda," she began in a low voice, "do you know that it's only half-past five? How naughty of you to come up here and shout!"

"Mummy—it's so perfectly lovely," said Belinda, putting her arm round her mother. "Other people are awake. Look, that long boat has just passed by and the little girl guiding it called out to me. And here comes another boat—without a horse this time, but with a motor inside to drive it. Chug-chug-chug—it makes rather a nice noise, I think."

Mummy forgot to scold. She sat there in the early morning sunshine with Belinda, watching everything. The water was a deeper blue now, and the golden patches were so bright that Belinda could not look at them.

The big fish went flashing by. More and more flies danced over the water and the swallows skimmed along by the dozen, snapping up the flies for their breakfast. The magnificent swan came back again, and looked at Belinda as if to say, "Is it breakfast-time yet?"

"Not nearly," said Belinda. "Though I'm most awfully hungry."

Mummy laughed. "I believe I can hear the others waking up," she said. "If so, we'd better all get up and I'll get breakfast. We can always have a sleep in the afternoon if we are tired. But really, this morning

is too   beautiful to waste even a minute of it."

Ann and Mike came up on deck, rubbing their sleepy eyes.   Ann cried out in joy when she saw the sparkling water and the waiting swan.

"Oh, you should have woken me too!   Mummy, isn't it lovely to know there's water under us, not land? Oh, do let's feed the swan. Where's Daddy? Daddy, wake up! You're missing something lovely!"

Then Daddy too came out in surprise, and sat down to watch the water and the swan, and the fish. They all watched the long canal-boats too, painted with so many bright patterns. Even the drinking-jars were painted, and the kettles and saucepans.

Some of the smaller children were tied with ropes, and once the children saw a dog on a barge, tied up with a rope too.

"He might fall in without being noticed,"

said Daddy, "and though he can swim, he would soon be left behind. So they've tied him up."

"Good morning to you!" called the canal-people politely, as they passed in their long boats, and each time the *Saucy Jane* bobbed as if she too was saying good morning.

"How early the canal-folk go to work," said Mummy. "I suppose they are up at sunrise and in bed at sunset. Well, if *we* get up at sunrise like this, our bedtime will have to be early too. Get dressed, children, and I'll cook breakfast. You lay the table, Belinda, and we'll have it out here."

It was a very early breakfast, but the children thought it was the nicest one they had ever had. The swan came up to be fed, and pecked up the bits of bread from the water. Once or twice he caught them in his beak when Mike threw some, and the children thought this was very clever.

"Well—we must get on with a few jobs," said Mummy at last. "And then, my dears, you are going to have a most important lesson. Daddy's going to teach you how to swim!"

6. A MOST IMPORTANT LESSON

THE children hurried to do the little jobs on the boat. Belinda helped Mummy to wash up. The dishes were put into the rack to dry. Belinda had to give them a polish with a cloth when she laid the table.

Ann made the beds, or rather the bunks. Mike took out all the bedding from his mother's bed, folded it tidily and put it into its cupboard. Then back into the wall went the bed, folding up neatly.

Daddy went to see if Clopper was all right, and to do a little shopping. Everyone worked happily. It didn't seem to be work, somehow! The sun shone down warmly, and the water glittered and sparkled. The swan sailed about round the boat hopefully, and drove away the two moorhens.

"I wish Daddy would come back," said Ann. "I want to swim across to the other side."

"You won't be able to swim at once, silly," said Mike. "It may take you a few days to learn. Look, lie flat on the deck, and I'll show you the strokes to use with your arms and legs."

But before Ann could do that, Daddy hailed

them from the shore. "Just coming! Are you ready for a swim?"

He was soon across and changed into swimming trunks, "Now," he said, "I'm going to dive into the water and swim past the boat. I want you all to lean over and watch how I use my arms  and legs. I shall use my arms like this . . . they will push away the water in front of me, and my legs will open and shut, so that I drive my body through the water. You must all watch carefully."

Splash! Daddy dived beautifully into the canal, and the children watched him. They could see his brown arms and legs moving strongly.

"I see how he swims," said Ann. "Look, he pushes away the water with his arms, and brings them back in front of him to begin all over again, and he opens and shuts his legs like a frog does when he swims. I'm sure I could do that!"

Mike was watching very closely. He lay down

flat on the deck. "'Watch me, Mummy," he said, and he began to do the same arm and leg strokes as Daddy. "Am I doing it right? Are these the strokes I should use?"

"Yes, Mike. That looks very good," said Mummy. "If only you can do that in the water, you'll do well. You lie down and do the strokes too, Ann and Belinda."

So they did, but Mummy said they were not as good as Mike. Then Daddy called to them. "Get on to the bank, and you'll find a nice shallow piece of water to step into. It will only be up to your waists, and you can learn your strokes there."

The three children climbed on to the bank. Then they slid down into the water. They were hot with the sun and the water was cold.

"Oooh!" said Mike, but he plunged himself right under at once. That was what Daddy always did, he knew.

"Oooh!" said Belinda, and waited a bit. She went in very slowly, bit by bit, not liking the cold water very much but determined to be brave.

"Good girl! Jolly good, Mike!" cried Daddy. "Come on, Ann!"

But Ann wouldn't go in any further than her knees. "It's cold!" she kept saying. "It's too cold!"

"It's warm once you're in!" cried Mike. "Baby Ann! Doesn't like the cold water! How can you learn to swim if you don't even get in?"

"Go on, Ann," said Mummy, who was now in the water herself, swimming along strongly. "Hurry up ! You look silly, shivering there."

It took Ann at least ten minutes to get in up to her waist. Daddy and Mummy began to teach Mike and Belinda, and they took no more notice of Ann.

"If she wants to be a baby, we'll let her," said Daddy. "Now, Mike, that's right—out with your arms—bring them back—out again. Good! Now try your legs. I'll put my hand under your tummy and hold you safe so that you won't go under. You can trust me. I'll be sure to tell you when I think you're doing well enough to take my hand away."

Mike got on extremely well. Soon Daddy took his hand away from under his tummy, and to his great delight Mike found that he could swim three strokes all by himself without going under.

"You'll soon be able to swim," said Daddy, pleased, and turned to see how Mummy was getting on with Belinda. She too was doing her best, and Mummy was pleased with her. But she would not let Mummy take her hand away, so they couldn't tell if she could really swim a few strokes or not.

As for Ann, she wouldn't even try! As soon as Daddy made her take her legs off the bottom of the canal, she screamed, "Don't! Don't! I'm frightened!"

"Well, you needn't be," said Mike. "Daddy won't let you go. You can trust him."

But Ann was silly and she wouldn't even try to use her arms in the way Daddy told her. So he sent her back to the boat.

"I'm ashamed of you," he said. "You must try again to-morrow."

After a while they all got out of the water and lay on the warm roof of the cabin to dry themselves in the sun. It was delicious ! Ann felt rather ashamed of herself.

"I'll try properly to-morrow," she told Daddy. "I really will."

"Well, little Ann, you can see for yourself that if you live on the water you must know how to swim," said Daddy. "I'll give you another chance to-morrow, and we'll see how you get on. Mike and Belinda will be swimming in a week's time—you don't want to be the only person in the *Saucy Jane* Family who can't swim, do you?"

7.   ANN HAS A DREADFUL SHOCK

THE happy summer days went by, and soon the family felt as if they had been living on the *Saucy Jane* for weeks! The weather was hot, the canal was blue and silver from dawn to dusk, and the swan became so tame that he hardly ever left the boat, but bobbed about by it all day.   All night too, Belinda said, for once when she had gone on deck in the middle of the night she had seen him sleeping near by, his head tucked under his wing.

Mike and Belinda could swim well now. Mike especially was a fine strong swimmer, and Daddy was proud of him.   But Ann was still foolish. She squealed when she first went into the water and always made a fuss.   And she wouldn't try to swim at all.

But one afternoon something happened that made her change her mind. Mummy was lying down in the cabin, glad to be out of the blazing sun. Daddy had gone to talk to a fisherman up the canal.   Mike and Belinda were on the bank at the back of the houseboat, lying in the cool grass.

Ann was playing with Stella, one of her best-loved dolls.   And quite suddenly Stella slid along the deck and fell overboard into the water.

Ann gave a squeal. "Oh, Stella ! Don't drown ! Keep still and I'll reach you with a stick!"

She got a stick and, leaning over the edge of the boat, she tried to hook poor Stella up to safety. But instead of doing that, she found herself slipping too, and suddenly into the water she went with a splash! She screamed as she fell, "Mike! Mike!" Then she could say no more, for she went right under the water and sank down, choking. She struck out with her arms, but she had not learnt to swim, and she was terrified.

"Why didn't I learn, why didn't I learn?" she thought, as she went down deeper. Water poured into her nose and mouth, she couldn't breathe, she couldn't do anything at all!

Mike heard the shout. He shot up from the bank when he heard the splash. He ran on to the boat, looked over the edge and saw poor Ann sinking down into the canal.

"MUMMY!" yelled Mike. "Ann's fallen in!"

Then the plucky boy jumped straight into the canal himself and tried to reach Ann. He found her, and tried to pull her up. In a terrible fright the little girl clutched him,

and began to pull him down under the water too.

Goodness knows what would have happened next if Mummy hadn't gone into the water too, and somehow got the two of them into the shallow part, where Mike could stand. He was gasping and choking. "Oh Mummy, she nearly drowned me."

Mummy carried Ann up on deck. The little girl's eyes were closed, but she was breathing. She had not been in the water long enough for any great harm to be done. She soon opened her eyes, choked, and began to cry with fright.

Mummy was very frightened about Ann's fall

"We daren't risk such a thing happening again," she said to Daddy, who was very upset too. "She won't learn to swim, so we shall just have to tie her to a rope."

Then, much to Ann's dismay, she had a rope tied round her waist all the time she was on the boat. Now, if she fell into the water, she could haul herself out. But Ann hated the rope round her.

"The canal-boat children laugh at me," she wept. "Nobody as old as I am is tied up. I

feel like a puppy-dog. Untie me Mummy, and I promise not to fall in again.

"I'm sorry, darling, but we can't risk it," said Mummy. "You're too precious. And, after all, you can always get rid of the rope yourself, if you want to."

"How?" asked Ann. "I can't untie this big knot."

"I know," said Mummy.   "I don't mean that.   I mean that you have only to be sensible and learn to swim and you will have the rope taken off at once."

"Oh!" said Ann, and she began to think seriously about learning to swim. After all, it had been dreadful sinking down into the water and choking like that. She shivered whenever she thought of it. And it did seem easy to learn to swim if only she would be brave and trust Daddy.

"How can you be brave if you aren't?" she asked Mike.

"I don't know," said Mike. "You might put it into your prayers, perhaps. You can always ask God for help in anything, Mummy says."

So that night Ann begged God in her prayers to help her to be brave enough to learn to swim, and made up her mind that she really would try.

And, of course, the very next day she found that once she let Daddy really help her, it wasn't so

dreadful after all!   She *could* be brave, she *could*
try—and soon, she would be able to swim!

Daddy was pleased with her. "You're just
as brave as the others now," he told her. "And
I do believe that you'll swim as fast as Belinda.
You've got such a strong stroke with your legs.
That's right—*shoot* your arms out—*use* your legs
well.   My word, I can hardly keep up with
you!"

Ann was pleased. "I did what you said,
Mike, and asked God to help me," she told
him. "It was much easier after that.   I'll soon
be able to swim as fast as you!"

Soon she was like a fish in the water, and
Daddy said she needn't have the rope tied round
her any more. The whole family went swimming
together, and presently Ann could actually swim
right to the other bank, have a little rest and
swim back again

"I've a family of fish !" said Daddy.   "Now
look out for waves—here come two barges!"

The children liked the waves. They lifted
their arms from the water and hailed the barges,
and the barge people shouted back.

"I wish we could go up the canal on a canal-
boat," said Ann.   "Oh, I really do wish we
could."

"Well, perhaps we can," said Daddy. "We'll
have to find out!"

8.   WHAT HAPPENED TO BEAUTY

DADDY had decided that it wouldn't be possible to go up the canal on the heavy old houseboat, which was moored flat to the bank. The children had been very disappointed.

"We needn't have brought Clopper then," said Ann. "He won't have anything to do. He'll be very bored."

"Well, maybe we can go on a canal-boat if we can find someone who will take us just for the trip," said Daddy.

But somehow it didn't seem to happen. Either the boats were taking coal, and Mummy said she didn't want them to go on a dirty coal-boat—or the canal-people didn't want to take them—or they just wouldn't stop long enough to discuss it.

Then one early morning a very strange thing happened just by the *Saucy Jane*. The children were all sitting on the houseboat roof watching the canal. They were waiting for a brilliant blue kingfisher who had fished near there the last day or two.

"He sits on that branch, watches for a fish,

then dives straight into the water and catches it." said Mike. "He's got such a strong beak."

It was while they were watching for the king-fisher that the strange accident happened.

A canal-boat, drawn by a slow old horse, came silently up the canal. A boy was guiding the boat, yawning sleepily. No one walked beside the horse, which plodded along the tow-path by itself, its head down.

"Even the horse looks half asleep," said Belinda. "He stumbles a bit now and again, look."

They watched the tired horse—and then, unexpectedly, it left the tow-path and walked straight into the water! It had fallen asleep as it walked and in its sleep had not known where it was going.

It went in with a terrific splash! Mike leapt to his feet, startled. The boy on the canal-boat gave a yell. "Dad! Beauty's fallen in. DAD!"

Then there was such a to-do! People poured up from the cabin of the canal-boat. The boat was guided towards where the horse was struggling in the canal.

"Oh, can he swim, can he swim?" squealed
Ann. " Oh, don't let him drown!"

But the horse had fortunately fallen into a
shallow part of the water, and after he had lain
in surprise on the mud, wide awake with shock,
he decided to get up.

He was very frightened, and it took three of
the canal-boatmen to quieten him and take him
from the water. They rubbed him down, and
one of them fixed a bag of oats
on his nose. When he felt it

there, he snuffled down into the oats
and began to eat. Then the men
knew he would be all right.

The children had watched the whole thing in
the greatest excitement. Fancy a horse falling

asleep and walking into the water! What a good thing he was all right.

The canal-boat was drawn up to the side. Everyone waited for the horse to recover himself and go on with his towing. But when he was set on the path again and coaxed to walk along it, he limped badly.

"Wait a minute," said one of the men, and bent to examine the horse's leg. "He's strained this leg. He won't be able to walk for a day or two, poor thing. It will never get better if we make him work now."

"Well, what about our load?" said another man, impatiently. "We've got to get that up to Birmingham before Saturday, It's important."

"We'll get a tug to tow us," said the first man.

Then Daddy, who had been listening and watching too, thought of a grand idea, and he called to the man.

"Hi! Do you want the loan of a good strong horse! I've got mine in the field there. You're welcome to use him for a bit if you like. He's longing for a bit of work."

The men pushed their boat out from the side, and soon she was lying by the *Saucy Jane*. Daddy and the men began to talk. The children looked with the greatest interest at the long canal-boat.

"Look at all the castles and hearts and roses painted on the sides of the boat," said Mike. "We've often seen them before, but we've never been able to look at them so closely as this. I wonder who painted them and why."

"All the canal-boats have them,'" said Belinda. "I wish I could get on this boat and look at every-thing. Even the tiller is painted, Mike. Just look."

"I say—listen to what Daddy is saying,'" said Mike suddenly, in excitement.

"Well," Daddy was saying, " you are welcome to borrow Clopper, my horse, if you like, and leave yours to rest in the field over there. He's a good strong horse, is Clopper."

"That's kind of you, sir," said the old boat-

man. "Er—how much would you be asking
us for the use of him?"

"Oh, I don't want you to pay me anything,"
said Daddy. "I'd be glad to have my horse
getting a bit of exercise."

"Well, sir—I don't rightly like taking your
horse and giving nothing back,'" said the old
man.

"Would you like to do something for *me*,
then!" said Daddy, and he smiled. "See
those three youngsters of mine! They badly
want to go up the canal for a trip—but this
houseboat of ours won't budge. You wouldn't
like to take us with you, would you?"

"Ay, that I would, if you don't mind putting
up with our rough ways," said the old boatman. "We'll be going through a few locks,
and the children will like to see those at work.
And we'll be passing through a long tunnel
too, bored in a big hill."

"Daddy, can we really go?" cried Belinda,
and she rushed up to her father. "It would
be grand. I do so want to travel up the canal
and see everything."

"Well, just for a day," said Daddy. "We'll
be ready in ten minutes, boatman. You can go
and get my horse while you're waiting!"

9. A DAY ON THE *HAPPY TED*

MUMMY quickly got ready a picnic meal to take with them, and told the children to get their macks just in case they needed them. The old boatman and his son went across to the field to get Clopper. Clopper came back with them willingly.

"I'm sure Clopper must feel as pleased and excited as we do!" said Ann. "I shall take Stella. She'll want to see everything too."

"I feel just like an adventure to-day," said Mike. "Goodness, fancy going up the canal—past villages and towns, through fields and woods, locks and tunnels !"

Clopper was tied to the tow-rope. The other horse, patted and petted, was left to graze peacefully in Clopper's field, and get over his shock. Everyone went on to the canal-boat.

One of the men went to walk with Clopper, for he had never been a tow-horse in his life. But he seemed to understand quite well exactly what to do, and he plodded along slowly and steadily.

The three children felt a little shy on the canal-boat at first. There was an old, rather fierce-looking woman there, but when she smiled she looked very kind. There were also three children, two boys and a girl, but they too seemed shy and hid among the boxes and crates that formed the cargo of the boat.

"It's called *Happy Ted*," said Mike, reading the name painted on the boat.

"Happy Ted was my grand-dad," said the old boatman. "He got this boat and my granny on the same day, and he called it *Happy Ted* after himself. Then my father had it, and now I've got it. And my son there will have it one day."

"Who paints all those lovely pictures everywhere!" asked Belinda, looking at the pretty castles and roses she saw on everything. "I do like them."

"Oh, I painted most of them," said the old man. "And my son he painted a few. All us canal-boat people paint our boats with hearts and castles and roses. It's our custom, and a very old one too."

"You've painted your big water-can, and your kettles, and this biscuit-tin too," said Ann. "And you've even painted a pattern down the handle of your broom and your mop !"

"Ah, we like everything to be bright and tidy." said the boatman's wife. "You should see my cabin."

"Can I?" said Ann, who was longing to peep into the tiny place where all the family seemed to live.

The old woman went backwards down the steps into the cabin. The children followed. There was hardly room for them to stand there all together, and certainly Daddy would have had to bend his head or he would have knocked it against the low ceiling.

But what a bright, lovely, little place it was! So tiny—like a dolls' house—and yet so many things in it that the children felt if they looked for hours they would never see them all.

There were a lot of brass knobs and ornaments hanging by the door. These glinted and winked like the sun, they were so bright and well-polished. Ann fingered one of them. "It's like a brass ornament that Clopper wears," she said. "Why do you have so many?"

"Ah, we canal-folk collect them," said the

old woman. "We like to see those brass things winking at us there. The better-off we are, the more we have. Don't you have any at home?"

"No," said Ann, making up her mind to collect as many as she could, and hang them just inside her caravan door when she got back to it at the end of the holidays. "Oh, look, Belinda, there's the little stove for cooking—and a table to sit at—but where's the bed!"

The bed was let into the wall in exactly the same way as the one in the *Saucy Jane*. On the wooden panel that shut it in was painted a bright pattern of hearts and roses. Mike wished he could paint like that. Perhaps Mummy would let him paint castles and things on the caravan door when he went back.

Everything was squashed into the small space of the cabin. The children could hardly believe that five or six people lived there all their lives!

"Fancy! You have your dinner here, and you sleep here, and on wet days you sit here!" said Mike. "It must be a dreadful squeeze."

"We like it," said the old woman. "I couldn't live in a house! What, be in a place that stands still all the time—that never hears the lap of the water, nor feels the swing of the waves! No, the canal-life's a grand life. We're water-wanderers, we are. You'll find us all up and down the canals, with our boats painted with hearts and roses and castles. We know the countryside like no one else, we know the canals and their ways, and we're proud of it!"

She looked at the children as if she was sorry for people who didn't live on a canal-boat. Land-folk! Poor things! What a boring life they must have, she thought.

It was hot and stuffy down in the little cabin, and Ann began to pant. They all went up the steps and out on deck. The long canal-boat was going smoothly through the water, with Clopper tugging her steadily.

"Good horse that," said the old man, taking his pipe out of his mouth. "Ay, a fine horse. He'll go a good many miles a day."

The children gazed ahead, and saw that the country rose uphill in front of them.

"How can we get the boat uphill!" asked Belinda, puzzled. "Look, we've got to go quite a long way up."

"We'll go through a lock soon," said the old boatman, smiling. "Then you'll see how a boat can go uphill! Ah, you didn't know such a thing could be, did you! But you'll see, you'll see!"

10. UPHILL IN A BOAT!

HOW can a boat go uphill? That was the question all the children were asking each other. Ann and Belinda did not know what a lock was, and Mike had only heard of canal-locks once or twice.

The *Happy Ted* went on and on, and Clopper's hoofs sounded just like his name as he plodded along. Then the old boatman pointed ahead.

"There's the lock," he said. " I'll tell you what happens, if you listen well."

The children were all ears at once.

"Now you see,"' said the old man, " the water above the lock is higher than below it. How are we going to get the boat up to the higher water?"

The children couldn't imagine. " Well, now," said the old man, "a lock is a small space, big enough to take one or two boats, between the high canal-water and the low canal-water. There are gates at each end, so that when a boat is in that bit of space, and both the gates are shut, she's sort of *locked* in. See?"

"Yes," said the three.

"Well, now," said the old man again, "the

gates at our end, the low-water end, are open, and we'll go straight into that bit of space there. Then we'll shut the gates behind us and lock ourselves in."

"What's the use of that?" asked Mike.

"Ah, you wait !" said the boatman. "Now comes the clever bit ! As soon as we're in that locked-up space, we're going to open holes in the gate in front of us. See? And water is going to pour through the holes, down into our locked-up bit of space. And that water is going to fill up the lock, and raise us up higher and higher and higher!"

"But what will happen when the water down in the lock rises as high as the water outside the gate!" said Mike.

"Aha! That's another clever bit !" said the boatman. "What do we do then but open the gates in front of us and there we are, on a level with the high-up canal, and we can sail out as easy as you like !"

"It's a marvellous idea!" said Mike. "Really marvellous!   Oh, I do want to get into the lock and see it all happen !"

"But what do you do if you're in a boat that's coming down from a high part of the canal to the low part ?" said Belinda.

"Easy!" said Mike. "*I* know that!   You just go into the filled-up lock, shut the gates

behind you and then open holes in the opposite
gate to let the water out and wait till the level
of the lock is the same as the low part; then
open the gates and out you go !"

"Right!" said the boatman. "Now you watch what
happens in a minute."

Clopper walked right up to the lock. There
was a steep bit of gravel for him to go up to
the higher lock-gate, and up he went. The
lower gates of the lock were open, and in went
the *Happy Ted*.

She stayed there, held by the tow-rope, which was now fastened round a big stone. The gates behind her were shut by the boatman's son. Then he and the old boatman went to open the holes in the gate in front—the "paddles," as they were called.

The children sat in the *Happy Ted,* shut up in the lock, waiting. Above them, behind other tall gates, was a great high wall of water. Somehow they had to get the *Happy Ted* up there so that they might sail out on the level again.

Water began to pour into the lock through the paddles of the gate. What a noise it made ! It was like waterfalls, rushing and gushing. The children felt excited.

"We're rising up, we're rising up! The lock is filling!" cried Belinda. "See that mark on the wall above us—now it's level with us-now it's below us, lost in the water, We're rising up, we're rising up!"

The lock was filled at last. The *Happy Ted* was much higher up than she had been before. She was level with the high part of the canal. She nosed against the top parts of the lock-gate and they swung open.   Out she went, drawn by Clopper, who was now once more pulling hard on the tow-rope,

"We're through the lock!   We're through! We've taken a boat uphill!" cried Mike. "It's wonderful! Are there any more locks soon?"

"Oh, yes—there's plenty just here," said the old man. "It's slow work, going through them. But if you're not in a hurry, why worry?"

"We're not in a hurry! We'd like this day to last for a whole week!" said Ann. "Oh, look

at those cornfields! They're getting golden already."

The canal-boat went slowly on through fields and woods, past pretty gardens, past lonely farm-houses. Sometimes it went by a small village where children came to wave. Once or twice it came again to a lock, and the children this time got out to help to open and shut the gates. It was lovely to watch the water pouring fast into the lock, filling it, bringing the *Happy Ted* higher and higher, until at last she could sail proudly out on the level again, much higher up than she had been before.

They went slowly by a dirty town. Here the canal was muddy and smelt nasty. The children didn't like it.

"Do people *have* to live in towns?" asked Ann. "Do they choose to?"

"Oh, lots of people don't like the country," said Daddy. "I'm glad you love it. Look at that busy yard over there. See the loads being put into the canal-boats, swung into them by the big cranes."

"How useful the boats are!" said Belinda, in wonder. "What a lot of heavy things they carry, Daddy. There are rail-roads and ordinary roads, and water-roads, aren't there? But I like the water-roads the best."

Out beyond the town they went, and in the distance stood a big hill. The canal ran straight towards it.

"We're going inside that hill," said the boat-man. "Put on your macks. It's cold and wet in there."

11.   A STRANGE ADVENTURE

"WE'VE taken this boat uphill—and now
we're going to take it *through* a hill,"
said Belinda. " It all sounds like magic.
I never knew things like this happened before."

"What happens to Clopper!" said Ann, suddenly.
"He won't like walking through a tunnel.
He'll be afraid."

"Oh, Clopper can't walk through the tunnel,
missy," said the boatman. "There's no tow-
path. He'll have to go right over the hill. My
son will take him."

"Are you sure you children want to go through
the tunnel?" said Mummy. "You may be afraid. It's so
dark and damp."

But all the children meant to go. What, miss
an adventure like this! Certainly not!

"How's the boat going to get through the
tunnel without Clopper?" said Mike. "It hasn't
got a motor to drive it along, like a motor-boat."

"There's a power-boat coming up behind,"
said the boatman. "He'll give us a tug. We'll
wait for him. You take Clopper, son!" he
called. His son leapt ashore, untied the tow-
rope, and disappeared up a steep grassy path

with Clopper. Ann pictured them walking right over the hill and down.

The power-boat came up. "'Hoy there!" called the boatman. " Give us a tug, will you?"

"Right!" called back the other man, and went on ahead. He caught the tow-rope of the *Happy Ted*, and made it fast to his own boat. Then, with a chug-chug-chug, his long canal-boat disappeared into the dark hole of the tunnel, and behind it went the *Happy Ted*.

How dark it was! Ann looked back and saw the hole they had come in by. It looked like a far-off speck of light now. Further into the tunnel they went and further. It grew darker still and the air was musty and damp.

The walls were dripping wet. It was some-how rather frightening and Ann cuddled up to Mummy, pulling her mack round her, for she felt very cold.

Suddenly she looked up and saw another tunnel right above her! She jumped in fright. "It's all right," said Mummy, "that was only an air-hole going right up through the hill to the top and coming out into the open air. We have to have a bit of fresh air here and there in this tunnel, you know!"

There were three or four air-holes and they were strange to look through. Far, far away at the top of them was a speck of light. Ann

Far, far away was a speck of light.

wished the tunnel would come to an end.

Chug - chug - chug- chug, went the motor of the boat in front, sounding oddly loud in the round dark tunnel. Chug- chug- chug- chug! Water trickled off the walls near by, and the canal looked deep and black. Nobody spoke at all.

Then Mike gave a cry that made everyone jump. "Look! What's that! That red thing gleaming in front of us, like a giant's eye!"

"Ah, that's only another boat coming towards us!" said the boatman. "Now listen, and you'll hear him tooting to tell us to keep to our side of the wall."

"Too-toot-tootoot!" came the call from the tug coming towards them. And the two canal-boats answered at once. "Too-too-too-tootoot!" Ann wished she could blow the strange trumpet that the old boatman blew.

Their boat and the tug that was pulling them kept close to their own side of the wall, scraping against it to let the other boat pass. Behind it came two more boats, full of goods. Bump-bump-bump. The boats scraped together now and again, for the tunnel was narrow.

Then they were gone, and the children saw only a faint light in the distance, getting smaller and smaller.

"I wish this tunnel would end," sighed Ann.

"I don't like it any more. It's too long. I like the locks better."

"You look out in front of you," said the boatman, and he pointed a h e a d . Ann looked—and to her delight she saw a round patch of daylight coming nearer and nearer.

"Hurrah!" said Mike. "We're getting to the end of it. Soon be out now !"

Cold and wet, the children at last came out into the blazing sunshine, and how they loved the feel of the warm sun on their heads and shoulders ! They flung off their damp macks at once.

The power-boat in front threw back their tow-rope to them, called good-bye and went off up the canal, chug-chug-chug-chug!

"There's Clopper waiting for us! " said Mike,

pleased. "I guess he wondered where we had all gone to. Clopper, you did better to go over the hill than through it!"

Once again they went on up the canal, with Clopper pulling well. How peaceful it was! How lovely to have a picnic meal on the deck of the long boat, sitting on the cargo, watching the green banks slip slowly by.

"Where are we going to sleep to-night!" asked Mike. "We'll never all get into that little cabin!"

"We're going back to the *Saucy Jane*, of course," said Daddy. "We can easily catch a bus. We'll be back in no time."

"In *no* time!" said Belinda, surprised. "But it has taken us all day to get here—and soon the sun will be going down!"

But Daddy was right. When they said good-bye to the canal-boat folk, and got on the bus, they were back at the *Saucy Jane* in an hour's time! How extraordinary.

"A canal-boat is a fine peaceful way of getting about," said Daddy, "but nobody could call it fast. Well, here we are at the dear old *Saucy Jane*. She looks pretty and peaceful enough, in the setting sun."

"We've had a lovely, exciting day," said Mike. "We may have gone at only about two miles an hour—but we've had time to see even the smallest flower at the edge of the water. Oh, I wish I lived on a canal-boat! I'll buy one when I grow up, and you girls can come with me and live on it. What a time we'll have!"

12.   GOOD-BYE TO THE
SAUCY JANE

THE holidays went by too quickly. August slipped away and September came in. Clopper had come back a long while ago and Beauty had gone back to work. All the children could swim like fishes, and each of them could row and steer a boat just as well as Daddy could.

The *Happy Ted* passed them once or twice more, and they always waved and called out their news. They knew other boats, too, and once they had gone off again for the day in another boat—but this time they had gone down the canal instead of up.

"I want to go downhill this time," Ann had said, so she had her wish. There was a tunnel on the way, but all three children had got out and walked over the hill with the horse. No more long dark tunnels for them! One was enough.

They had learnt many things besides swimming, diving and boating. They had learnt the ways of the wild creatures of the water, and had grown to love the great long-legged herons that sometimes visited the canal, and the white swans who now came to be fed every morning.

They were all brown and strong. Their legs and arms were sturdy with swimming and rowing. Daddy and Mummy were proud of their three children.

"It was the best holiday we could have chosen for them!" said Mummy." The very best. They've been good children, helpful and sensible and kind —and what a lot they've learnt."

It was sad to have to think of leaving the *Saucy Jane*. But now the evenings were getting chilly, and often low mist came over the water that made the children shiver.

"I don't want to go, though," said Ann. "I want to stay all the year round, Mummy."

"You wouldn't like it, Ann," said Mummy. "You are not a child of the canal. You would shiver and get cold and be miserable. It is all right for the summer—but now that the autumn is coming, we must get back to our cosy caravans."

"And there's school, too," said Mike. "I like school. I want to play games again with the other boys and read my books and do carpentering."

"I like school, too," said Belinda. They all went to boarding-school, but each week-end they returned to the caravans. And how cosy those caravans were in the winter-time, when the curtains were drawn, the lamps were lighted, and the stove glowed warmly! Games and books and television—yes, winter was good as well as summer.

They cleaned the *Saucy Jane* well. Belinda scrubbed the decks and made them spotless. Ann helped Mummy to turn out all the neat cupboards. Mike and Daddy repainted the little boat that belonged to the Saucy Jane.

"Auntie Molly will ask us again if we leave her houseboat better even than we found it!" said Belinda. "Mummy, do you think she will?"

"I shouldn't be surprised," said Mummy.

"Well fancy, we have only broken one cup and one plate, and those I have managed to replace. And except for the ink that Mike spilt on the rug I really don't believe we have done any damage at all."

"I'll pay for the rug to be cleaned," said Mike, and Mummy said yes, he could. Once that was done, the boat would be as perfect as when they first came aboard.

They packed their things into the two trunks they had brought with them. They locked up the *Saucy Jane*, and Mike took the key across to Mrs. Toms. She was sorry to see them go.

"I've got fond of the *Saucy Jane* Family !" she said. "I'll miss you. Come again next year !"

The car came driving up and everyone got in. Daddy had already gone off with Clopper, riding on his back. Everybody felt a little sad.

"Good-bye, *Saucy Jane*," said Mike. " We did love living in your little cabins, sunning ourselves on your white deck, and feeling you bob up and down on the little waves !"

"Good-bye, swans," said Ann. "I'm afraid you won't get bread for your breakfast to-morrow. But I expect Mrs. Toms will feed you if you go to her."

"Good-bye, canal!" said Belinda. "I've loved every minute of you and all the wild things that belong to you, and the long painted boats that slide over you day by day. Good-bye."

"Now don't let's get miserable about saying good-bye," said Mummy. "We may no longer be the *Saucy Jane* Family, but we shall soon be the Caravan Family again—and we shall say 'hallo' to the two caravans, and to dear old Davey and Clopper!"

Off they went in the car. Nobody said a word for a little while, because they were all thinking of the happy *Saucy Jane*. But then they began to think of the caravans.

"I can collect the wood each day for our fire, Mummy," said Mike.

"I can fetch eggs and butter from the farm," said Ann.

"I can keep our caravan tidy and clean like I used to," said Belinda. "Oh, Mummy-won't it be fun to be back again in our houses on wheels! One for you and Daddy and one for us children! I'm longing to see the caravans again."

And how lovely they looked when they did see them. There they stood in a pretty field, all newly painted, clean and bright. The children tumbled out of the car with a shout.

"Hallo, caravans ! We're back again. Hallo, darling Davey, have you missed us? Clopper and Daddy will soon be back!"

Soon the fire was going and Mummy was cooking their first caravan meal. It was good to be back after all. Daddy was pleased to see such smiling faces when be arrived on Clopper.

"Hallo, Caravan Family !" he said. "It's a funny thing, but you're JUST as nice as the *Saucy Jane* Family !"

And he was right about that, wasn't he?